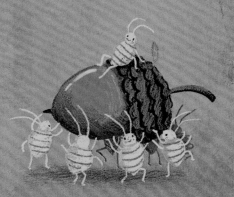

Copyright © 2020 Clavis Publishing Inc., New York

Originally published as *Goedenacht en slaap zacht*
in Belgium and the Netherlands by Clavis Uitgeverij, 2019
English translation from the Dutch by Clavis Publishing Inc., New York

Visit us on the Web at www.clavis-publishing.com.

Good Night, Sleep Tight written and illustrated by Esther van den Berg

ISBN 978-1-60537-588-5

This book was printed in May 2020 at Neografia, a.s., Su ianska 39A, 038 61 Martin-Priekopa, Slovakia.

First Edition
10 9 8 7 6 5 4 3 2 1

Clavis Publishing supports the First Amendment and celebrates the right to read.

Esther van den Berg

Good Night, Sleep Tight

"Hi, I'm Dot.
I'm checking to see
who is ready for bed.
Are you?"

Clavis
NEW YORK

Here comes Dot.
She's arriving at the Bug Hotel, just in time for bedtime.
Before Dot goes to sleep, she'll make sure all the other
bugs are getting ready for bed.

reception

KNOCK-KNOCK!
Dot knocks at the first door.
It's Dung Beetle. He's getting ready to take his bath.

Dot needs a bath too, so she jumps in and joins Dung Beetle.
When they both are nice and clean, it's time for Dot to move on.

"Good night, sleep tight," she calls.

KNOCK-KNOCK!
Dot wraps on the next door.
It's Stick Bug. She's busy picking out her pajamas.

"I think I'll wear the striped ones," says Stick Bug.
"Those look great on you," Dot tells her.
Dot picks out pajamas too.
With dots, of course.

"Good night, sleep tight."

Dot flies over to the next door.
RING-RING!
It's Fly.
"What are you doing to get ready for bed?" Dot asks Fly.
"I'm going to brush my teeth. Care to join me?"

Dot and Fly brush up and down and back and forth.
Then they spit the toothpaste into the sink.
Patooey!

"Time for me to go," says Dot.
"Good night, sleep tight."

TAP-TAP at the next door.
Pill Bug is on the toilet.

"It's always a good idea to pee before bed," thinks Dot.
So she hops on the toilet next to Pill Bug.
Whoosh!

She flushes and flies off.
"Dry night, sleep tight."

RING-RING!
Who is Dot going to visit next?
It's Bookworm.
Bookworm always reads a book before bed.

Actually, Bookworm reads lots of books before bed!
Dot can't read yet, so she just looks at the pictures.

"Good night, sleep tight."

Finally, Dot arrives at her own door.

✓ Bath? Check.

✓ Pajamas? Check.

✓ Brush teeth? Check.

✓ Toilet? Check.

✓ Bedtime story? Check.

Everyone is ready for bed,
and now Dot can go to bed too.

But there's a tapping on the door.
KNOCK-KNOCK!
Five bugs poke their heads through Dot's door.
"We forgot something, Dot. We all need a . . .

". . . good-night kiss!"

Sleep well, Dot.
Good night . . .

... sleep tight!

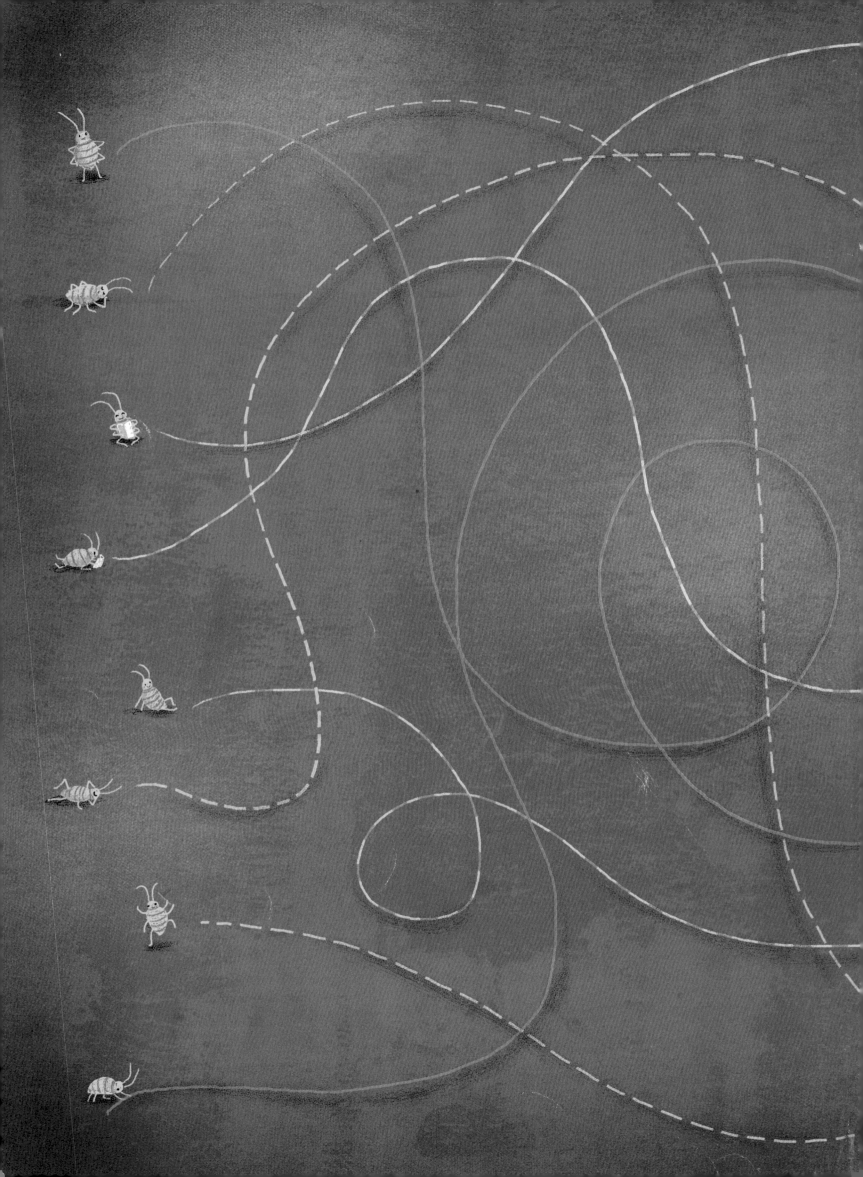